19 MAY 2010

-8 OCT 2013

1 9 JAN 2019

0 2 FEB 2019

D0345827

Please return/renew this item by the
last date shown to avoid a charge.
Books may also be renewed by phone
and Internet. May not be renewed if
required by another reader.

LONDON BOROUGH

K124

For Dave the dentist, with love.

Evans Brothers Limited
2A Portman Mansions
Chiltern St
London W1U 6NR

First published 2004

Text copyright © Evans Brothers Ltd 2004
© in the illustrations Anni Axworthy 2004

British Library Cataloguing in Publication Data
Moffatt, Julia
    Open Wide! . - (Zig zags)
    1. Children's Stories
    I. Title
    823. 9'2 [J]

ISBN 023752791X

Printed in China by WKT Company Limited

Series Editor: Louise John
Design: Robert Walster
Production: Jenny Mulvanny
Series Consultant: Giu Matthews

ZIG ZAG

Open Wide!

By Julia Moffatt

Illustrated by Anni Axworthy

Evans

Today was Danny's first visit
to the dentist.

Danny didn't want to go.

His brother Tom had told him
all about it.

The dentist was a big, scary
monster, who lived in a dark,
spooky cave.

He had a screechy drill to scare little children.

Danny never, ever wanted to go to the dentist.

He hid under his bed.

"Oh, there you are!"
said Mum.

"I don't want to go!"
said Danny.

"Everyone has to go to the dentist," said Mum.

"I feel poorly," said Danny.

"Fibber," said Mum.

Inside, Danny was surprised.

It didn't look like a spooky cave at all.

The dentist didn't look
like a monster, either.

"Would you like a ride on my chair?" he said.

"Wheeeee!" said Danny.

23

"Open wide!" said the dentist.

"Perfect, Danny. Remember to keep brushing!"

The dentist gave Danny
a sticker.

"This is fun!" said Danny.

"Can we come back
tomorrow, Mum?"

Why not try reading another ZigZag book?

Dinosaur Planet   ISBN: 0 237 52667 0
by David Orme and Fabiano Fiorin

Tall Tilly   ISBN: 0 237 52668 9
by Jillian Powell and Tim Archbold

Batty Betty's Spells   ISBN: 0 237 52669 7
by Hilary Robinson and Belinda Worsley

The Thirsty Moose   ISBN: 0 237 52666 2
by David Orme and Mike Gordon

The Clumsy Cow   ISBN: 0 237 52656 5
by Julia Moffatt and Lisa Williams

Open Wide!   ISBN: 0 237 52657 3
by Julia Moffatt and Anni Axworthy